Littlenose

More adventures of

Littlenose

Littlenose The Hero

Littlenose
the Hunter

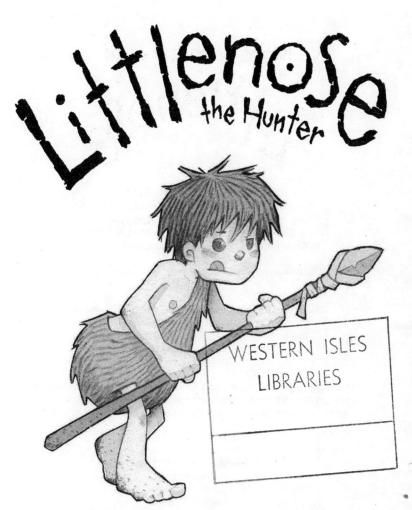

WESTERN ISLES
LIBRARIES

JOHN GRANT
Illustrations by Ross Collins

SIMON AND SCHUSTER

SIMON AND SCHUSTER

Littlenose the Hunter was first published in 1972
Littlenose the Fisherman was first published in 1974
The other stories were first published in 1976
in Great Britain by The British Broadcasting Corporation

This edition published by Simon & Schuster UK Ltd, 2006
A CBS COMPANY

1 3 5 7 9 10 8 6 4 2

Simon & Schuster UK Ltd
Africa House
64-78 Kingsway
London WC2B 6AH

A CIP catalogue record for this book is available from the British Library

ISBN 1-416-91090-5
EAN 9781416910909

Typeset by Ana Molina
Printed and bound in Great Britain by Cox & Wyman Ltd, Reading, Berkshire

Contents

Littlenose the Hunter

Littlenose was a Neanderthal boy who lived long ago, when people lived in caves and hunted animals for their food. When he grew up he was going to be a hunter like his father.

So, early one morning, Littlenose and Dad hurried off to an open space in front of the caves. All the hunters of the tribe and several other boys were there. A small stout man with white hair was in charge of the boys. He had been a very great hunter once, and now he was their teacher.

First the apprentice hunters were made to stand in a line while the teacher inspected their equipment.

Littlenose was carrying a satchel made of animal skin, and the evening before he had packed it very carefully with the things he needed. There was a clean pair of furs, a bundle of dried twigs, two flints, and a flint knife. And a brightly-coloured stone. He didn't really need the stone, but it was nice to look at.

Littlenose held his satchel out, trembling. The teacher raised one bushy eyebrow at the coloured stone, but nodded approval. Littlenose glowed with pride.

At last the party set off in single file. They followed the river to begin with, then crossed a ridge, and later a winding trail led them down into a thickly-wooded valley. At long last they halted in a wide clearing.

Dad and the other men didn't stop. They marched on across the clearing, and in a few minutes had disappeared. Then, one by one, the teacher called the boys to him. One was sent to catch fish. Another had to find fruit. A third was to look for bracken to make soft sleeping places for the night.

Littlenose was last to be called.

"Now, Littlenose," said the teacher, "I have a very important task for you. You will prepare our fire. Listen carefully. This clearing will be our camping place for the night. At sunset we shall require a good fire to cook supper. You must light a fire which is big enough to burn all afternoon. We don't want a great blaze, but a bed of hot ashes." Here he paused and wagged a finger at Littlenose. "If the fire isn't right, then that will mean a late supper, and hungry hunters are very impatient people. Now, it won't take you all day to build a fire. Everyone is going to gather on the other side of the hill, there." And he pointed. "At midday we eat, and then start lessons."

"Yes, sir," said Littlenose.

"I'll see you at midday, then, on the other

side of the hill. Just follow the path." And he strode off, leaving Littlenose all alone in the clearing.

Littlenose looked about him. He'd better get started. He made his preparations with great care. First, he gathered a pile of dry sticks, then took out the knife and the twigs and flints from his bag. He whittled the twigs into bundles of shavings, then struck the flints together, until sparks fell on them. Most of the sparks went out right away, but at last one stayed alight long enough for Littlenose to blow it gently. The spark grew brighter until it was a pale, flickering flame. Quickly he built more twigs into a pyramid over the flame, and blew again. Soon the twigs were crackling and spitting. He took out the coloured stone and admired it for a moment before putting all his things back in the bag. But the fire was supposed to be big enough to last until nightfall. Littlenose began throwing branches onto the flames. Soon he had to fetch more branches from the woods. The fire grew bigger and became higher and hotter. Littlenose wiped the sweat from his eyes. Surely *that* would be enough to last?

Littlenose took one last look at the fire, which was now making shimmering heat waves in the air, and followed the path into the forest. He could see the top of the hill behind which he was to meet the others, and the path led straight towards it. But soon it began to turn away to one side.

"This is no good," thought Littlenose. "I'll be quicker if I leave the path and make straight for the hill." And at first he was. There was very little undergrowth and walking was easy. He was quite close to the foot of the hill when he came to a sudden stop. There was water in front of him – it stretched black and smooth and deep-looking right to the bottom of the hill. This, of course, was why the path had not taken the straight route. Littlenose picked up a large stone and threw it. The stone fell with the hollow splash that stones make falling into deep water. He couldn't possibly get across here, and to go back to the path would take too long. He walked along the bank throwing stones.

He was beginning to think that the water sounded quite bottomless, when he paused. That last stone had sounded different. He tried another at the same place. It made the definite rattle of a stone falling into shallow water – shallow enough for him to wade to the other side. He splashed across, and in a few moments was safely on the other bank at the foot of the hill.

By the time Littlenose scrambled up the hillside and over the top to find the others, he was hot and tired. He was glad to sit down with the other boys and eat a lunch of cold grilled fish and berries. It was when he took out his knife to cut his fish that he made an awful discovery. His coloured stone was gone! But he hadn't time to look for it. Already the teacher was getting ready for the first lesson.

The boys were made to sit on a log and the teacher drew with a charred stick on the smooth surface of a large rock. He started off with a lecture on animal tracks. He sketched here, pointed there, and from time to time tapped on the rock with his pointer. He talked very rapidly in a high-pitched voice, and Littlenose began to feel more and more drowsy. He began to daydream of being such a fine hunter that he could go out before anyone was awake and be back with a rabbit, a red deer, a rhinoceros and an elk by breakfast time.

Littlenose sat up with a jerk. The teacher was speaking.

"Come along, now," he exclaimed angrily. "Surely *someone* can tell me what those tracks are. You, there!" And he nodded towards Littlenose.

Still half-dreaming, Littlenose blurted
out, "Rabbit, red deer, rhinoceros and elk."

"Well done. Well done," exclaimed the
teacher. "You seem to be the only one who
has paid attention. YOU will be tracker on
our hunt this afternoon. Who knows? You
may even find us a rabbit, a red deer, a
rhinoceros and an elk."

The men rejoined the party for the hunt,
and Dad glowed with pride when he
learned of Littlenose's success. Once more

they formed a long line, but this time Littlenose was in the lead. "Come on, Littlenose," said the teacher. Littlenose held up his hand and waved the party forward. He led them under low bushes and branches until their backs ached, and made them squeeze through narrow spaces that bruised their ribs. The men soon realised that there were disadvantages in having a small boy as a tracker.

Actually, Littlenose had no idea where

he was going – he just reckoned that they were bound to see some sort of animal sooner or later, and then he could say that that was the one he was tracking. He led the party out into a clearing. He was hot and tired, so he held up his hand, and they all stopped. He put his finger to his lips, and the hunters held their breath and waited expectantly.

Across the clearing was a jumble of rocks. They looked shady and cool; Littlenose made his way towards them. The hunters tiptoed after him. They waited as Littlenose crept inside.

The next moment the hunting party scattered like leaves in the wind. Head over heels they tumbled towards the trees as, with an earth-shattering roar, there stepped out from among the rocks an enormous lion. It had been sleeping peacefully in the shade when Littlenose blundered in and fell over it. By the time the lion's eyes became accustomed to the bright light, there was not a hunter to be seen.

They ran and ran, straight down the hill. But they could still hear the lion roaring.

"Look," said Littlenose, pointing. "It's getting foggy. If we can hide in the fog, the lion won't see us."

Sure enough, a haze was drifting through the trees, and was beginning to form dense streamers between the trunks. In a few moments the hunters were only dim shapes in the mist. The next time they heard the lion roar it was a long way off. It had lost them. Again they stopped, and at almost the same moment everyone said, "This isn't fog!"

They had been so busy running that they hadn't noticed what their noses and smarting eyes now told them. It was smoke! It was getting thicker every moment.

"A forest fire," cried one man. "Run!" And he set off up the hill, away from the smoke. Then he remembered the lion, and ran back. "What shall we do? What shall we do?" he cried.

"Leave it to me," said Littlenose, and he began to climb a tall, straight fir tree. The smoke grew thicker the higher he went, but suddenly he came out of it, and saw blue sky above him. He also saw the fire. The whole forest seemed to be ablaze, particularly the site where he'd built the camp fire. The camp fire! He'd done it again! Well, they'd wanted a big fire! Anyway, it was too late to worry about that now. But there wasn't much time. They had to get away from the trees before they caught fire *and* avoid the lion. Littlenose hurried to the ground.

"Quick, follow me," he shouted. "Hurry!"

Again the hunting party scrambled along behind Littlenose. Only a few more paces, he thought; then he stopped dead. In front was a wide, dark and deep-looking stretch of water. They had circled round, and had reached Littlenose's earlier short-cut.

"We'll never get across. We're trapped!" the hunters cried.

"No, there is a way," shouted Littlenose. And he dashed along the bank, trying to recognise a tree or a bush or something which would give him a clue. Suddenly, everyone nearly fell over Littlenose as he bent down and picked up something from the ground.

"This is the place," he cried, and dashing into the shallow water he splashed his way to the far bank.

Littlenose looked at what he held in his hand. Wasn't it lucky that he had lost his coloured stone as he crossed the water the first time? If he hadn't spotted it lying in the grass, they would never have found the crossing place in time. In a few moments, the whole party was safe on the bare hilltop, while the fire raged in the woods. All night, the hunting party crouched in darkness, watching the flames below. In the early hours of the morning it began to rain, and at last the sun rose on a soggy, sooty and sizzling stretch of blackened woodland.

Black, wet, weary, and smelling of wood smoke, Littlenose arrived home with Dad late in the evening.

"It was all Littlenose's fault," said Dad to Mum that night. "I know he saved us, but it was only because of him that we *needed* saving. Look at him, sound asleep there without a care in the world."

Littlenose lay in a corner of the cave curled up under his fur covers. And in his hand he clutched a brightly-coloured stone.

Two-Eyes' Revenge

The cleverest and kindest person in the
whole Neanderthal world was Littlenose's
Uncle Redhead. At least, Littlenose thought
so. He had already given Littlenose a flint
knife, a picture of a beaver drawn on a
piece of bark, and a set of pipes for making
music. But, on this particular occasion,
Uncle Redhead had been with the family
for nearly a whole day and had so far given

nothing to Littlenose.

It was evening, and Littlenose sat with his parents and Uncle Redhead around the remains of the evening meal. Everyone was too full to talk much, and soon Mum began to clear away the supper things. Dad bent over the fire, and poked it into a blaze. Uncle Redhead just sat with a faraway look. Littlenose just sat.

Dad was giving the fire a last poke when suddenly he leapt up with a yell.

"Ouch!" he shouted. "What was that? I've been stung!" And he rubbed his arm. Then he yelled again and jumped up, this time holding his ear.

"There are too many insects about," he shouted. "I'm going in." And he stamped angrily into the cave.

When Dad was out of sight, Uncle Redhead

almost fell off his rock laughing. He clutched his sides as he chortled into his beard. Favourite uncle or not, Littlenose thought him pretty heartless. After all, Dad had had two very painful stings, which was no laughing matter.

Mum came out of the cave on her way to the river carrying a large bowl. Uncle Redhead pointed to her, and suddenly there came a loud PING! from the bowl, which Mum almost dropped in surprise.

"Careful!" said Uncle Redhead, as Mum

went on her startled way. And again he doubled up with laughter.

Poor Littlenose was thoroughly bewildered. He turned to Uncle Redhead, but Uncle Redhead just said, "Time for your bed, young man. Pleasant dreams. See you in the morning." So Littlenose went to bed, a very perplexed boy.

In the morning, Littlenose tried desperately to ask his uncle about the strange happenings of the night before. But Uncle Redhead didn't appear to notice him, and chatted casually to Mum and Dad through breakfast.

However, when they had eaten, Uncle Redhead said, "Come on, Littlenose. Let's go for a walk. I still have to give you your present."

They walked off into the woods together, and there Uncle Redhead stopped on a grassy bank.

"Can I have my present now?" asked Littlenose.

"Just a moment," said Uncle Redhead.

He reached across and picked a thin, straight stick about the length of his hand.

"It's a berry-shooter," said Uncle Redhead. "It's a rowan stem, and, see, it's hollow."

But Littlenose still didn't understand.

With a sigh, Uncle Redhead took the hollow stick again, and putting a hand into a pocket, produced some red, wrinkled berries and put them in his mouth.

"Goodness, he *must* be hungry," thought Littlenose.

But Uncle Redhead did not chew the hawthorn berries. He put the berry-shooter to his lips, made a noise like "pfft!" and sent a berry shooting up into the leaves over their heads. Again and again and again he did it. "Pfft! Pfft! Pfft!"

"Oh, now I see," shouted Littlenose excitedly. "Let *me* blow one. *I* want to try."

Uncle Redhead gave him the berry-shooter and a berry. "Put the berry in your mouth," he said, "and put the berry-shooter to your lips. Take a deep breath."

Littlenose did as he was told. Then he gave a startled gasp. "I've swallowed the berry!" he gasped.

"That's all right," said Uncle Redhead. "I've plenty more." And he handed him another. This time, Littlenose got it right, and the berry popped out of the end of the tube and landed at his feet.

"Not bad," said Uncle Redhead. "Try again."

Littlenose tried again. And again. And again. In fact, he practised all afternoon, and by the time they set off for home he was getting very good.

"Now," said Uncle Redhead, as they approached the cave, "you must promise to be extremely careful when you are playing with your berry-shooter. I don't want you getting both of us into trouble."

When Littlenose awoke next morning, Uncle Redhead had gone. But tucked in amongst the furs under which Littlenose slept was the berry-shooter and a good supply of dried berries.

Littlenose couldn't wait to play with his new toy. He slipped a berry in his mouth and blew it towards Mum, who was busy preparing breakfast. But the berry flew over her head and she didn't even notice it. However, Littlenose remembered Uncle Redhead's words about being careful, and decided to wait until he was up and about before trying again. As soon as breakfast was over, he went to practise. But shooting at leaves and flower heads was pretty dull. He tried aiming at a fat thrush perched on a branch. What Littlenose didn't see was a wasps' nest hanging from the branch. Instead of hitting the bird, the berry smacked straight into the wasps' nest. Out came the wasps, and off ran Littlenose as fast as he could.

The wonderful toy was not turning out to be as much fun as he had hoped. People were much more interesting targets than leaves or birds . . . or wasps' nests, for that matter. After all, Uncle Redhead hadn't actually *forbidden* him. He had only said to be careful. And he would be. Nobody had caught Uncle Redhead playing tricks with the berry-shooter, and they wouldn't catch *him*.

Unfortunately, Littlenose was not Uncle Redhead. He just wasn't cunning enough. He couldn't keep his face straight, and roared with laughter every time one of his hard berries hit someone on the ear or the nose, making them jump. It was not long before everyone in the tribe had been hit at least once; and one day some of the neighbours complained to Dad.

"Have you still got that berry-shooter?" he asked Littlenose, when they had gone. Littlenose nodded. "Right," said Dad. "Because it was a present, you may keep it; but you must on no account shoot it at people. One more complaint, and it goes in the fire. Right?"

"Yes," said Littlenose, very relieved that he still had his toy, but wondering what use it was going to be now.

At this moment Two-Eyes came ambling along. Two-Eyes! Of course! Why hadn't Littlenose thought of it before? He was Littlenose's best friend, but he wasn't "people". Not ordinary "people", anyway.

As Two-Eyes settled himself in a warm patch of sun to doze, Littlenose let fly with a berry. And Two-Eyes didn't move. Littlenose tried again. Two-Eyes didn't even look up. Then Littlenose realised that Two-Eyes just couldn't feel the hard hawthorn berries through his thick fur.

There was just one part of Two-Eyes which had no fur. The tip of his trunk. Littlenose took careful aim, and blew.

"Pfft!"

With a loud squeak, Two-Eyes leapt up.
Littlenose blew again, and this time the
berry hit Two-Eyes in the ear.

From that day on, Two-Eyes had no
peace. He had only to show himself for a
moment to find a stream of berries flying
round his head. At length, thoroughly
disgusted with things, he went off to stay
with some friends, where, at least, he was
safe from Littlenose and his berry-shooter.

When Two-Eyes had gone, Littlenose felt very sorry for himself. He had no one to shoot berries at, and he had no one with whom to do all the exciting things that he and Two-Eyes did together. He tried shooting at twigs floating in the river, and at fish swimming below the surface. But it was much too dull. Soon the berry-shooter was forgotten, and Littlenose wished that Two-Eyes would come back. And, one day, as summer was drawing to a close, Two-Eyes came trotting into the cave.

"Two-Eyes, you've come back!" cried Littlenose, happily. And he threw his arms around the little mammoth and hugged him. Once more, Littlenose and Two-Eyes played together. They explored the woods, paddled in the river, and invented games.

Littlenose had certainly forgotten the

berry-shooter. The Neanderthal folk had very short memories, and Littlenose's memory was shorter than most. But Two-Eyes was a mammoth. A mammoth not only *looked* like an elephant: like an elephant, a mammoth *didn't* forget. And a mammoth could be very patient indeed.

Summer was almost over. The leaves were beginning to turn red and gold. One morning, Littlenose called to Two-Eyes, "Come on, Two-Eyes, let's go and gather fruit." Together, they ran off into the woods, and in no time found all kinds of fruit, ripe and ready for eating. There were raspberries and blackberries and Littlenose gorged himself on those, and then he saw clusters of crab apples. He scrambled up the tree and threw down handfuls of the small apples. Two-Eyes picked one up, but immediately spat it out again. It was sour and unripe. Littlenose jumped down to the ground and ate several before he, too, decided that perhaps they were not quite ready for eating.

On another tree, dark clusters of elderberries showed among the leaves. Once again, Littlenose climbed into the branches and shook them. The tiny, dark fruits showered down onto the ground over Two-Eyes, who was waiting below. As they did so, an idea began to form in the little mammoth's mind. At last he was going to have his long-awaited revenge. Reaching down with his trunk, he began sucking up the fallen elderberries. Then he hid in a clump of bushes, and waited.

A moment later, Littlenose climbed down from the elder tree. He looked around him

. . . but there was no sign of Two-Eyes.

"Two-Eyes," he called. "Where are you?"

The reply he got took him completely by surprise. Two-Eyes stepped out from behind the bushes, took a deep breath, and with his trunk pointed out straight in front of him, sprayed Littlenose with elderberries.

"Oh! Ouch! Stop it, Two-Eyes," cried Littlenose, his hands in front of his face. But Two-Eyes didn't stop. He kept up a steady stream of small, hard berries until his trunk was empty, and then, breathless, but laughing mammoth laughter, he ran off to the river to wash the sticky elder juice from his trunk. Littlenose ran after Two-Eyes, but gave up after a short distance, and leaned against a tree to get his breath back. He felt rather dizzy. He didn't feel at all well. The woods seemed to be going round and round. He decided that it must have been the crab apples. Two-Eyes had sensibly spat his out. Why couldn't he have? Feeling very sick and dizzy, he made his way along the path towards home. It was dark when Littlenose reached the cave, and Dad was just thinking of going to look for him.

"Hurry up," called Mum. "I've kept supper for you."

At the mention of supper, Littlenose felt even worse. "Oh, no," he said. "I feel awful. I just want to go to bed." And he lay down in his own corner and pulled some furs over himself.

"What have you been eating?" asked Dad.

"Crab apples," groaned Littlenose.

"I might have known," said Mum. "You'll never learn. Let this be a lesson to you this time. You'll probably feel better in the morning."

In the morning, Littlenose woke, feeling well, and ravenously hungry. He bounced out of bed, but as soon as Mum caught sight of him she cried, "Get back to bed this minute!"

"I feel fine," said Littlenose. "Only hungry."

Mum had already shouted to Dad, who came running. He took one look at Littlenose. "What is it?" he said. "I've never seen anything like it. Does it hurt? Do you feel hot? Or cold?"

"I feel fine," said Littlenose. "I want my breakfast."

"Breakfast?" said Dad. "Don't tell me that

you feel fine, with spots like those."

"Spots?" said Littlenose, and he looked down. His arms and body were covered with a rash of purple-red spots.

"We must get the doctor," said Mum.

"No, we won't," said Dad. "All *he* does is put a fancy mask on, shake a lot of old bones over your head, charge five green pebbles, and tell you to stay in bed for a week. Tell him to see Auntie. She's bound to have medicine for this sort of problem, and she doesn't cost anything."

Auntie was a strange old lady who lived in a cave some distance from the others. Auntie always seemed to be ill herself, which Littlenose thought strange for someone who was supposed to be able to cure others.

When Littlenose and Mum arrived, Auntie was sitting by the fire with a fur rug over her knees.

First Mum had to give Auntie a lot of local news. It was mainly about people who had broken their legs, or had been eaten by something, or had been struck by lightning.

Finally, Auntie turned to the patient. She made him turn around. She looked in his ears and down his throat. Then she fetched a skin bag and a clay bowl from the back of the cave. She mixed something from the bag in the bowl with a little water and, handing it to Littlenose, said, "Drink. All of it."

It looked and smelt horrible, but Littlenose took a deep breath and drank. It tasted even worse than it looked or smelt, but he got it all down, coughing and spluttering so that he

spilt most of it over himself. He handed
back the cup, and wiped himself with his
hand. Then he saw the others staring at
him.

"It's working already!" cried Mum.

Littlenose looked down. Where he had
spilt the water, the spots were disappearing.
He rubbed some more, and they vanished,
leaving a purple stain on his fingers.

Wonderingly, he touched his fingers with his tongue. The taste was slightly sweet. He licked some of the spots on his arms. Yes. He knew what it was, and he laughed and laughed.

"It's elderberry juice," he shouted. "Where Two-Eyes shot them out of his trunk at me. I must have had the spots when I came home last night, but it was too dark to see."

A rather embarrassed Mum led Littlenose out of the cave after a muttered "goodbye and thank you" to Auntie.

But Littlenose paid little attention to either of them. He was hurrying home to have the biggest breakfast he could eat.

The Great Journey

At the time when Littlenose lived, almost
the worst thing that could happen was to
become ill. And this was because there
were no doctors in those days. At least,
there were no doctors as we know them. A
Neanderthal doctor wore a ferocious mask
and carried a stick hung with beads which
rattled when he shook it.

Instead of having his hand held and his

temperature taken, the Neanderthal patient
was more likely to have magic signs painted
on his forehead and the beaded stick shaken
over him to drive away the sickness. About the
only thing which was the same as today was
that the medicine often tasted terrible! Some
very odd things went into the making of it,
although it was mainly herbs.

Now, despite all this,
the doctor was a very
important member of
the tribe. He came
somewhere between the
Old Man and the
Chief Hunter. One
good thing about
being doctor to a
tribe was that
other people had to work

for him. It was supposed to be an honour. The most usual thing was to be sent to gather herbs to make the medicine. The women and children of the tribe were used to going out to collect the common herbs. But, for his most special medicines, the doctor required the leaves of the yellow bogweed which grew far, far away. Finding it was no job for women and children – it was work for the hunters.

One day, Dad came home looking irritable. The doctor had told him he needed more yellow bogweed.

"Oh no!" said Mum. "That only grows beyond the Great Moss. It will take weeks. Must *you* go?"

"Not only must *I* go," said Dad, "but Littlenose must come too. He is officially an apprentice hunter, and must take his turn with the rest."

At the mention of his name, Littlenose looked up. "What's that?" he said. "Are we going hunting again?"

"No. Gathering plants," said Dad, "for the doctor."

"Picking flowers!" exclaimed Littlenose. "That's girls' work. I thought I was learning to be a hunter."

"We are not going picking flowers," said Dad patiently. "We are going to one of the most dangerous places in the world. We must not only travel to the Great Moss, we must cross it. Only on the far side can we find the yellow bogweed."

"Can't we just walk round the Moss?" asked Littlenose. "Like we do the bogs on the moor?"

Dad flung up his arms. "Have you *no* imagination, Littlenose?" he cried. "The

Great Moss stretches far away on either side. No one has ever seen the ends of it. It takes days to cross from one side to the other."

"Cross?" said Littlenose. "You said I must never try to cross a bog. It's dangerous. I might be drowned."

"The Great Moss," explained Dad through gritted teeth, "is not just an ordinary bog. It is a huge swamp. It lies in the flat lands northward towards the Ice Cap. Parts of it are bog. Parts are almost dry land, with trees growing. There are streams and ponds, and thickets of reeds that you could get lost in. It is a damp, sad place, full of mist and the noise of water. Even the birds and animals sound unhappy. And, the land where the yellow bogweed grows is also the hunting ground of the Straightnoses."

Now, the Straightnoses were the deadly

enemies of the Neanderthal folk. They were tall, straight-nosed, and incredibly clever. Littlenose began to think that perhaps he would be better off doing girls' work picking flowers. The next few days were busy getting ready for the journey. Then, in the grey light of an early morning, they set off. Just before they started, Mum handed Littlenose a tightly-rolled skin bundle.

"I made this for you," she said. "Dad will show you how to use it."

Littlenose was puzzled, but he slung it on his back with his other gear, kissed Mum goodbye, and followed the men down the trail.

It was the longest journey which Littlenose had ever undertaken. And it was not only the longest, it was the most pleasant . . . at least to begin with. As they were not hunting animals, there was no need to look for tracks, and no particular need even to be quiet. The hunters trudged along in twos and threes, chatting, laughing, and occasionally singing. Littlenose chased butterflies, and threw his boy-sized spear at imaginary bears.

On the eleventh day after leaving home, the holiday came to an end. They had barely started their morning's march when one of the hunters pointed, and cried, "Look!"

Everyone looked. At first Littlenose could see nothing. The grassland they were crossing rolled away under a grey, heavy sky. There was no wind. Not even a blade of grass moved. Then Littlenose, peering where the man pointed, saw a thin line on the grey sky.

"What is it?" he asked.

"Smoke," said Dad. "A long way off."

"That means people," said another hunter.

"Either some of our own folk or . . ."

"Straightnoses!" gasped Littlenose.

"Exactly," was the reply. "And if we can see the smoke of their fire from here, then it must be a big one. This is no small party. This is a whole tribe on the move. One of ours. Or one of *theirs*."

"But," said Dad, "the Straightnoses don't usually hunt or travel in this part of the country. We shouldn't meet them until we've crossed the Great Moss."

"That just proves what I've always said," went on the first man. "The Straightnoses are unreliable. We must be on our guard from now on."

Luckily there were no emergencies during that night. They started off again after breakfast, and it was not long before Littlenose began to sense that something was different. The sky was still grey, but seemed lower. The air was definitely colder. They were now walking on damp grass, and ground that sometimes squelched underfoot. They passed stagnant ponds, and often they had to wade through long stretches of shallow water.

Two days later, towards late afternoon, Dad pointed ahead. "There they are," he said. "We'll soon be there."

"There are what?" said Littlenose.

"The trees," said Dad. "We'll make our last camp there before crossing the Moss. This is just the edge of it. Tomorrow we do the difficult bit."

Littlenose looked ahead, and could just make out a dark blob in the mist. The trees, when they reached them, turned out to be a group of ancient willows. They grew on a little island of raised ground, but even here the earth was damp and chilly. Dad came over to him.

"You must be very careful, now, Littlenose,"

he said. "And do exactly as you are told. First, hang your things up clear of the ground."

Littlenose did this, slinging his gear from a stump of tree branch.

"Now," continued Dad, "you are Fire Boy. You must get a fire lit while we work."

Littlenose wondered what the work could be, but he set about collecting firewood. Most of it was damp, and some of it was very wet. At first the fire was all smoke, but gradually, some flames appeared.

The men finished their work. One had been fishing, and a fine fish supper was set grilling over the fire. The others, however, seemed to have been doing something very strange. They had cut bundles of long, straight willow twigs which they had then stripped of their bark. Littlenose wondered of what use they could possibly be, but before he could ask, someone shouted, "Time to eat!" Some of the men stood to eat. Some squatted. Nobody sat – the ground was too wet. Littlenose wondered where they would sleep.

The meal over, Dad said, "We've a hard day ahead of us tomorrow. It's time to get some sleep."

"On the wet grass?" asked Littlenose.

"No, in our hammocks," replied Dad.

"But I haven't got a hammock, whatever that is," said Littlenose in a bewildered voice.

"Yes you have," said Dad. And he lifted down the bundle which Mum had given Littlenose. Dad untied it, and Littlenose saw that it was a long wide strip of skin with rawhide ropes at each end. Dad tied the ropes on one end to the trunk of a tree. Then he stretched out the skin and tied the other end to a second tree. The skin now hung clear of the ground.

"That," said Dad, "is your hammock. Get in." And he lifted Littlenose up. The hammock swung gently, and was very comfortable indeed. Across the glade, other hammocks were being slung, and in a few moments the whole party was snug and dry and calling "Goodnight" to one another.

Littlenose looked up. A few stars had appeared. As he watched, the stars seemed to blink. He watched, and they did it again.

"How very odd," he thought. Then he saw why. The hammock was swinging gently, and he was seeing the sky through the branches of the willow tree. It was the twigs and leaves coming in front of the stars that made them seem to blink. Littlenose wriggled so that the hammock

swung faster. This was fun. He swung faster
and faster, while the stars blinked and winked
furiously. Then he swung just a little too
far. With a yell and a thump he tumbled to
the ground. Immediately, the camp was in
an uproar. Men grabbed for their spears,
and Littlenose found himself in the middle

of a circle of very unfriendly faces.

"I fell out," he said.

"You were fidgeting," said Dad. He lifted Littlenose back into the hammock and wagged a finger at him. "One more piece of nonsense from you, and you sleep on the ground. All right?"

"All right," said Littlenose, and he lay down and fell fast asleep.

The hunters set off very early next morning. Each man carried his spear and a small bag to hold the special leaves for medicine. In addition, each held a bundle of the peeled willow sticks. The hunters moved in single file, and quickly reached the edge of the Great Moss. It was just as Dad had described it. A sad, lonely place; just marsh and bog. The line of hunters stopped and then started again. Littlenose, bringing up the rear, saw one of the white twigs sticking upright in the soft ground. Dad called back to him, "Keep to the line of sticks, otherwise you will be drowned. We must feel our way across, and these will show us how to get back."

Peering ahead, Littlenose could see the leading hunter prodding the ground carefully in front of him with his spear. Only when he found firm footing did he move forward. Every so often, he stuck in a willow twig to mark the route, and slowly and steadily the little party zigzagged its dangerous way across the Moss. Behind them, a winding line of white sticks showed where they had passed. Half the day was gone before the last stick was pushed in, and they were walking on dry turf up a gentle slope.

After a pause for a rest and something to

eat, the plant picking began. The yellow flowers of the bogweed were easy to spot, but it was the thick fleshy leaves which the doctor required. It was back-breaking work. Littlenose was luckier than the others in that he didn't have so far to stoop. All the same, he was glad when he had filled his bag with leaves and could straighten up. He looked all around. It was a very depressing spot. Then a movement caught his eye. It was near a low ridge of land a short distance off. Was it a large animal? A mammoth, perhaps? He saw a line of small shapes, dark against the grey sky.

He watched for a moment longer, then dashed over to Dad.

"Look," he said, pointing.

Dad looked, dropped flat into the grass and whistled softly. At his signal, the others

also dropped into cover, and watched where
he pointed. The shapes were coming closer.
They were men. Tall and erect, carrying
spears, and getting nearer every moment.

"Hunters," said Littlenose.

"Straightnoses," said Dad. "We must get
out of here fast."

"When I give the word," whispered the
leader, "make a run for it. Follow the
willow twigs. Don't try taking short-cuts."

He took a last look towards the
Straightnoses, then shouted, "NOW!" and
raced helter-skelter for the Moss. The rest

followed. Littlenose found himself bringing up the rear once again, as he slipped and stumbled over the quaking ground from one stick to the next. They were well into the Moss before they paused for breath. Then they had a terrible surprise.

Neanderthal people were not very bright, and they had imagined that crossing the Moss would somehow bring them to safety. But, to their horror, the Straightnoses were doing as they were, and following the sticks. In panic, the hunters fled on. Except Littlenose, that is.

"How silly can we get?" he thought.

Running to the nearest twig, he pulled it out, then he ran after the hunters, pulling out each twig as he came to it, and throwing it into the Moss so that no one could tell where they had been.

Very quickly a gap grew in the trail.
When the Straightnoses reached the last
willow stick they shouted with rage. One
tried to dash after Littlenose, and was only
saved because another grabbed him by the
hair as he sank into the marsh. A
Straightnose threw a spear which hit the
ground behind Littlenose with a plop and
vanished.

Disappointed, the Straightnoses turned
back towards solid ground.

When the Neanderthal hunters reached

their camp, Littlenose was treated as a hero. After all he had saved them from the Straightnoses. He was allowed to sit in his hammock *and* swing in it, while the fire was made by one man and his supper brought to him by another.

When they reached home, many days later, he was again treated as a hero. Littlenose wasn't sure how long it would last but one thing was certain – he was going to make the most of it!

Littlenose the Fisherman

Although Littlenose was an apprentice hunter,
and often went with the men of the tribe to
hunt, the Neanderthal folk didn't eat meat
all the time. They had wild fruit, roots and
bulbs, nuts in the autumn, and honey in
the summer. And in spring, when the ice
had vanished from the ponds and streams,
the Neanderthal folk became fishermen.

One day, Littlenose's father announced

that it was time Littlenose was taught to fish.

"But he can't keep still!" said Mum. "He's so noisy every fish will disappear when Littlenose reaches the river."

"I know," said Dad gloomily, "but he must learn. Starting tomorrow."

Neanderthal fishermen needed to be very quiet and patient as well as skilful. They would crouch by the river bank or wade into the shallows, stay very still, and when a fish appeared lunge down with their special fishing spears.

First Dad tried to teach his son how to use a fishing spear on dry ground. But Littlenose became confused and managed to spear his own foot. It didn't hurt much, luckily, because he'd made such a bad job of sharpening the spear.

Next day Dad took him on a real fishing

trip. All morning Littlenose waited quietly and watched Dad, who was patient and careful, and, one by one, caught six trout.

"Now it's your turn," said Dad. "Do as I did, and you can't go wrong."

Littlenose lay on the bank until his head and shoulders were over the water and took a firm grip on the spear.

"Whatever you do," whispered Dad, "don't let go of the spear."

Littlenose waited; a fisherman must have patience. He peered into the water until a wide open mouth and dark body shot towards the surface. Then he plunged downward with his spear as hard as he could. Too hard! He lost his balance and, with a yell and wildly-kicking legs, fell headlong into the water.

Calmly, Dad caught him by the hair and

pulled him onto the grass. It was minutes before Littlenose could recover his breath. Then he held up the spear and said proudly, "I didn't let go!"

Back at the cave, Mum wrapped Littlenose in a warm fur rug, while Dad sat muttering to himself.

Suddenly, Littlenose looked up. "Dad," he said, "I've been thinking."

Dad laughed. The idea of Littlenose thinking was very amusing. Mum was somewhat taken aback, too, but she said, "Go on, Littlenose. Tell us."

"Well," said Littlenose, "Dad went to a lot of bother just for six trout. I've got a better idea."

"I suppose you could do better," snorted Dad. "Let's hear this wonderful idea, then."

"Catch bigger fish," said Littlenose.

"Eh?" said Dad.

"Yes," said Littlenose. "If those trout had been six times as big you need only to have caught one."

Dad sat for a moment with his mouth hanging open then he laughed and laughed. The tears rolled down his cheeks. He couldn't speak. "Oh ho!" he shouted. "All we need is one giant trout and our troubles are over!"

"Not trout," said Littlenose. "Salmon."

Dad stopped laughing. "Now you're not being funny," he said. "Just plain silly."

"No, I'm not," said Littlenose. "We've had salmon to eat before."

"Just think for a moment," said Dad. "Every spring the salmon pass up the river from the sea. You've seen them. They're as big as you are. They leap and race through the water as fast as a galloping buffalo. They stay right out in the deep water. They don't come near to the surface waiting to be speared. They're much too clever! The ones we've eaten were injured and washed up on the sand. Nobody catches salmon."

"But Uncle Redhead told me . . ." began Littlenose.

"Uncle Redhead tells you far too much," said Dad. "Mainly nonsense!"

Dad didn't care much for his brother-in-law. He thought he was more clever than was proper in a Neanderthal man.

"Uncle Redhead says," continued Littlenose, "that the bears catch salmon. Upstream the river becomes very rocky, with rapids and little waterfalls. The bears wade out to the rocks and catch the salmon as they rest, or as they jump clear of the water. Uncle Redhead says the ones we get are those that the bears couldn't keep hold of and that are washed downstream by the current."

Dad said nothing for a moment, then he nodded his head wisely. "All we have to do, then, is grow claws like the bears, wade into the river and pick out as many salmon as we need. Littlenose, you're impossible!" And he walked out of the cave in disgust.

"Never mind, dear," said Mum. "I think it's

a perfectly lovely idea, but it's time for bed."

Littlenose spent most of the night lying awake thinking. Dawn was breaking when he did fall asleep, but by then his plans were made.

No one mentioned fishing at breakfast, and when Littlenose strolled out of the cave with Two-Eyes his pet mammoth, Mum didn't even notice that he was carrying his hunter spear and some food. Littlenose had given a lot of thought to the matter of a spear. Fish spears were light and delicate for catching small fish, but to use one on a salmon would be like throwing stones at a woolly rhinoceros. Littlenose had his own spear, a real hunting spear, but boy-size.

Littlenose decided that Two-Eyes had better come to help him carry his catch. Even one salmon was likely to be too big for Littlenose.

Soon Littlenose and Two-Eyes had left the caves behind, and were in strange country. Few of the tribe ever ventured farther than this, and Littlenose imagined that any moment he would come to the place where the bears fished.

The sun rose higher, Littlenose trudged on, and still the river flowed wide and smooth.

At midday he stopped by the water's edge and had a picnic. Even as he sat and ate, salmon could be seen far out in the river. The great fish were leaping head and shoulders out of the water and falling back in showers of spray. The sun glinted on their scaly bodies, and Littlenose wondered how he could ever hope to catch one. But sitting looking wasn't going to do much good. If he didn't reach the rocky place soon he would have to go home empty-handed.

The afternoon wore on.

Littlenose and Two-Eyes were by now very tired. Several times they had to leave the river bank to make their way around the cliffs and marshes, and Littlenose hoped that they hadn't missed the bears' fishing place. But soon he realised they were not going to reach their destination that day, and it was too late to go home. There was only one thing to do. He found a sheltered corner between two rocks, and lighting a fire with his flints to keep away wild animals, he snuggled down against Two-Eyes' shaggy coat for the night.

Littlenose woke with the birds' dawn chorus, and had the remains of his meat. Two-Eyes ate some grass, then the two of them continued their journey. The river swung round a bend at this point, and as they turned the corner Littlenose cried, "Look, Two-Eyes!"

Below, the river narrowed, and in the gap between the banks were several large rocks around which the water swirled and frothed. As they watched, a salmon leapt high out of the water, over the rocks, and into the smooth river upstream. Then another salmon splashed its way up one of the small waterfalls, almost completely out of the water.

Without wasting any time, Littlenose climbed down the bank and made for the slippery rocks, while Two-Eyes watched. By the time he reached the middle of the river he was breathless. He found a rock that was fairly flat, and carefully stood upright. Gripping his spear, he waited. Nothing happened. There were no salmon. The last one must have gone!

Suddenly a movement caught his eye. There were salmon all around him! Only the occasional fish leapt above the rocks. Many more were swimming through the channels between the boulders. Looking down, he could see huge dark shapes weaving their way past the rocks. Now and again one would break the surface, and Littlenose had a glimpse of large eyes and great hooked jaws.

He waited no longer. Trying to remember all that Dad had told him, he gripped his spear firmly, took careful aim, and struck downwards with all his strength.

A jarring shock almost broke his arm, and next moment he was in the river. He clung on to the spear as it was wrenched this way and that. He was buffeted and bruised by a large tail and dragged hither and thither through the water. Then he was clutching something, and the river was carrying him along, sometimes on top, but more often under the surface.

It seemed hours later that Littlenose felt sand under him. He shook the water from his eyes and staggered ashore . . . dragging behind him the most enormous salmon. It was quite dead, and he could see where his spear had struck, but of the spear itself there was no sign. There was also no sign of Two-Eyes. He would have to get his fish home all by himself.

Meanwhile, back at the caves, a search party had just returned.

"There's no sign of him," said the leader. "We can't think of anywhere else to look. Do you have any ideas?"

"No," said Mum, sobbing, "he was such a good boy, never any trouble."

"Probably been eaten," said a neighbour. "It's always happening." He broke off as one of the hunters ran up.

"This has just come down with the current." He held out a boy-sized hunting spear.

"It's Littlenose's," wailed Mum. "He was talking of catching a salmon, and now they've eaten him."

For the rest of the day, the tribe watched

the river as if waiting for Littlenose himself to come floating by like the spear.

"If only he hadn't gone off by himself," they said. "There wasn't a nicer boy in the whole tribe. He was so kind! So generous! Always willing to help. Never disobedient. An example to everyone."

Their hopes were raised when late in the afternoon Two-Eyes came wandering along, for usually when he arrived Littlenose was not far behind. But when night fell there was still no sign of Littlenose.

Suddenly, the silence was broken by a voice shouting, "Hi! Come and help me, somebody!"

The tribe poured out of their caves, wondering what all the fuss was about.

A small figure, dripping wet and covered

with mud and fish scales, was dragging
something heavy along the river bank.

"Littlenose!" they all screamed. "Where
have you been? We've been worried sick.
You're a wicked inconsiderate boy, with no
thought for others. You ought to be thoroughly
ashamed." They calmed down a bit when
they saw the huge salmon, but went off
muttering about modern youth.

Mum cried a little. Then she washed

Littlenose and tucked him up in bed.

Dad carried the salmon into the cave, and, do you know, by the end of the week Littlenose didn't like salmon any more!

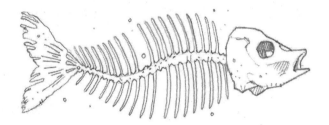

Littlenose's Holiday

Littlenose was bored. He scuffed the sandy floor of the cave with his feet. He sighed and picked up a twig and started to whittle it, then threw it into the fire and sighed again.

"For goodness' sake, stop fidgeting," said Mum. "Go out and play. It's a beautiful day."

"I've nothing to play at," said Littlenose.

"Play with Two-Eyes," said Mum.

"He doesn't want to play. He just wants

to sleep," said Littlenose.

"Well, go out and play by yourself," said Mum impatiently. "In fact, just go before you drive me completely mad!"

Wearily, Littlenose rose and dragged himself out into the sunshine. What could he do? Climb a tree? Climb one, he thought, and you've climbed the lot. Paddle in the stream? Last time he had fallen in and had been scolded for getting his furs wet. Idly, he picked up a broad grass blade, held it flat between his thumbs, and blew. It made a squeaking noise. Littlenose brightened up. He picked a better grass blade and blew harder, then again and again. His boredom forgotten, Littlenose took an enormous breath and blew with all his might, making a wild shriek that was pure joy to his ears.

Next moment he was
knocked sideways
by a hard cuff on
the side of the head.
Dad stood over him.

"What do you think
you're doing?" he shouted.
"Disturbing the whole
neighbourhood like that!"

Dad took Littlenose by
the ear and marched him away from the
caves. "If you must make that ghastly
noise," he said, "at least make it where we
can't hear it." Then he went back to
apologise to the neighbours.

Littlenose dropped the blade of grass.
There didn't seem much point in it now.
Anyway, he might as well do something
useful, like practising fire lighting.

He collected a handful of twigs and dry leaves, and after only three attempts managed to catch a spark on one of the leaves. The fire soon crackled briskly, and Littlenose glowed with satisfaction.

Now he thought he would try something more difficult. When hunters were troubled by flies and midges in their camp they made a smudge, a very smoky fire which drove insects away. The trick was to put green stuff onto a fire without actually putting it out.

Littlenose piled on handfuls of grass and the smoke began to get thicker. Soon it was coiling in dense wreaths. He kept adding more greenery, and from time to time he knelt and blew into the heart of the fire just as he had seen the hunters doing. Soon it was lunch time and Littlenose decided to hurry home before he got into more trouble.

Mum was very relieved when Littlenose arrived, smelling a bit smoky, but smiling. They were just finishing their meal when there was a cough, and one of their neighbours appeared. He shuffled his feet, cleared his throat and said, "I don't want to complain, but could I have a word with you for a moment?"

Dad nodded, and the man came in, followed by his wife.

"It's like this," said the man. "The wife, here, washed her best white fur wrap and hung it on a bush to dry, and it seems that your boy, there, was lighting fires or something. Anyway, he was making a lot of smoke and, well, have a look for yourselves."

The woman held out a grey, grubby piece of fur. It was spotted with what seemed to be soot, and couldn't have looked less like a best white fur wrap. Moments later,

Littlenose was in bed in disgrace, Mum was offering to re-wash the fur wrap, and Dad was vowing to feed his son to the first black bear that snuck its nose out of the forest.

Before going to bed that night, Dad was in despair. "I wish I knew what to do with Littlenose," he said. "He's more trouble than a whole herd of woolly rhinoceros."

"I thought you were going to feed him to

a black bear," said Mum.

"Attractive as the idea is," said Dad, "it is illegal."

"I'm sure you'll think of something," said Mum.

Next morning at breakfast there was suddenly a cheery shout from outside. Littlenose brightened up immediately. "That's Uncle Redhead," he cried.

Sure enough, the stocky figure of his uncle could be seen coming up the path. He waved. "Any breakfast left?" he shouted.

"If you hurry," called back Littlenose, as Mum hurried out to greet her brother. Dad didn't come out.

After Uncle Redhead had eaten, he said, "I really came here to ask you a favour."

Father looked at him carefully and said, "Mm."

"It's like this," said Uncle Redhead, "I've some business to take care of here, and I could do with help. A sort of camp boy to fetch and carry, and to light the fire. Do you think that Littlenose could be spared for a couple of weeks?"

Dad leapt up and shouted with delight: "Two weeks? You can have him for two months if you want."

When Littlenose heard that he was to go with Uncle at first he was too thrilled to speak. Then he hugged his uncle and demanded, "When do we go?"

Littlenose and Uncle Redhead left in the early afternoon, and by sunset were far from home. Littlenose was busy lighting a fire under a big tree, and Uncle Redhead had gone off to catch some fish for supper. Soon four fish were grilling over the flames.

When they were eaten, to Littlenose's delight, Uncle Redhead brought out from his pack two pieces of honeycomb dripping with honey.

Littlenose had never had so much honey at one time before. He sat munching before the fire while his uncle told marvellous tales of the strange places he had visited and exciting things he had done. Littlenose hoped they were going to do something exciting on *this* journey.

Soon it was time for bed, and after building up the fire to keep away wild animals, they settled down for the night. For a while Littlenose lay awake and wondered what they would do in the morning. What did happen came as a shock.

He was wakened by shouting. "Wakey, Wakey! Rise and shine! Show a leg! The sun's burning your eyeballs!"

Littlenose opened one eye. The sun was barely over the horizon, and the air felt chill. He snuggled down under his fur covers, but they were pulled off by Uncle Redhead.

"Come on now, time's a-wasting. Follow me," he shouted, and ran off at a rapid jog-trot. Littlenose got up and followed. He was soon out of breath and had a stitch in his side. Then, to Littlenose's relief, Uncle Redhead stopped and waved him on. They were beside a broad stream.

With a cry of "Last one in's a woolly mammoth!" Uncle Redhead threw off his furs and leapt into the icy water. Littlenose was horrified. He stared as his uncle splashed about calling, "Come on in, the water's lovely!" Slowly, Littlenose took off his furs and stood on the edge, goose-pimply and shivering. He stuck one foot timidly into the water. With a shout of glee, Uncle Redhead grabbed his ankle.

Next moment Littlenose was gasping and spluttering in the icy stream. He made for the bank, missed his footing, and fell headlong.

"That's the stuff," said Uncle Redhead. "Get the water right over you. Enjoy yourself! I always look forward to my morning dip."

All Littlenose was looking forward to was getting out of the freezing water.

Littlenose felt warmer, if completely breathless, by the time he had run to camp. Uncle Redhead was already cleaning some fish. "Hurry up with the fire, Littlenose," he said, and Littlenose blew the smouldering ashes into a flame. The fish were quickly cooked and eaten, and afterwards Uncle Redhead again gave him a huge piece of honeycomb. Fed and dry and glowing all over, Littlenose thought that perhaps life with Uncle Redhead wasn't too bad after all. He stretched out beside the fire, feeling pleasantly drowsy. But not for long.

"Mustn't hang around," said Uncle Redhead, kicking sand onto the fire to smother it. "There's work to be done." Before Littlenose realised what was happening they were on their journey again.

Uncle Redhead walked with long strides

which made it difficult for Littlenose to keep up. He hummed and whistled as he went, and from time to time burst into song. Or else he started long conversations. But Littlenose was too breathless to do more than whisper the occasional reply. They stopped briefly at noon for a quick snack of fruit and honeycomb. Littlenose was too tired to ask where they were going. He just trudged behind his uncle, who laughed and sang as merrily as ever, and never seemed to get tired at all.

At long last they stopped. They were on the shores of a small lake, and made their camp by a clump of pine trees. Littlenose flopped wearily to the ground. But it was his job to make the fire.

By the time that the fire was burning up, Uncle Redhead had come back with two fat rabbits. Quickly he cut them up and set them to roast over the flames. Littlenose ate his share with relish. He sat back, full, and his uncle grinned and said, "Now here's the bit you've been waiting for, isn't it?" And he handed Littlenose a piece of honeycomb. Littlenose groaned. He thought he would burst, but somehow he managed to chew and swallow the sweet, crunchy wax.

That night again Uncle Redhead laughed and chuckled his way through the same old stories, occasionally breaking into song. Littlenose just wanted to sleep. He began to think how nice it would be if his uncle would only be quiet for a while! At long last he said goodnight and pulled the covers over himself. Thankfully, Littlenose settled down to sleep too, without much success. Uncle Redhead even talked in his sleep. He muttered to himself, and from time to time let out a guffaw of laughter.

Yet that was not the only thing keeping Littlenose awake. He remembered the dip in the icy stream, and dreaded the morning. There seemed no way of getting out of it, and at last he fell asleep determined to show Uncle Redhead that he was tough too.

It seemed only a moment later that he heard: "Wakey! Wakey! Rise and shine!"

Without a moment's hesitation, Littlenose was out of bed. Down the beach he ran, off came his furs and he hurled himself into the lake. He landed with a thump. The water was only a few inches deep and the bottom was black, smelly, mud!

Littlenose sat among the slime, while

Uncle Redhead roared with laughter. "If I'd known you were so keen on bathing I'd have warned you about the lake," he roared. "Never mind. Get yourself cleaned up, and I'll get breakfast ready."

After much painful scrubbing with handfuls of grass, Littlenose was rid of the mud, although he still smelt a bit. He cheered up until Uncle Redhead produced the honeycomb and broke off a generous piece for him. "Good, eh?" he said as Littlenose forced himself to eat it. "Now you'll feel better."

Littlenose felt slightly sick.

The journey continued for the next few days, and Littlenose gradually learned to ignore his uncle's chatter. To his relief none of their overnight camps was near a suitable bathing place. But the supply of honey seemed endless, and Littlenose wondered how he could ever possibly have liked it.

It was exactly a week after leaving home that Uncle Redhead said, "Early to bed tonight. We've work to do tomorrow." What the work was he wouldn't say, but in the morning Littlenose was set to making a parcel of the flints which Uncle Redhead carried in his pack. Even Littlenose could see that these were the very best, top-quality flints, which were always difficult to come by.

After they left camp, they headed for a patch of forest. Then they paused on the edge of a clearing, and Littlenose's hair stood on end with fright. In front of them was a camp. It was quiet, and everyone seemed asleep. But it was not a Neanderthal camp. From the skin shelters slung between the trees, Littlenose knew that this was the camp of a tribe of Straightnoses. He was terrified, but Uncle Redhead led him around the edge of the clearing to a huge tree. Part way up the trunk was a hole, like an owl's nesting hole. Uncle Redhead reached into the hole and took out a small pouch. He replaced the pouch with the parcel of flints. Then, with a careful look around, he led the way back to their own camp.

Littlenose was still shaking with fright as they packed for the long journey home. But Uncle Redhead was as cheery as ever. "It's a good season," he said, as he looked at the coloured pebbles in the pouch.

"These people really know a good flint when they see one. I'm thinking of retiring soon."

"But that was a Straightnose camp!" said Littlenose.

"Of course," said his uncle. "They're good customers. Some of my best friends are Straightnoses. But they're a bit shy of us.

They think the Neanderthal folk are dangerous."

Littlenose could make nothing of all this. He felt they were lucky to have escaped in one piece.

The return journey was as bad as that coming. They marched for miles every day, most mornings started with a cold bath, and Uncle Redhead never stopped talking. There was honeycomb every day, and before they reached home Littlenose had toothache.

Two-Eyes trumpeted with joy when he saw Littlenose, and Mum cried and kissed him. Dad wasn't sure whether he was pleased or not.

As for Littlenose, he was so glad to be home that he wasn't bored again.

For almost a week, at least.

Bigfoot

One day, Dad told Littlenose that they
were all going to spend a holiday with some
of their relatives. Littlenose didn't want to
go. And said so.

"You'll do as you're told for once," said
Dad, "and like it."

"All right," said Littlenose, adding under
his breath, "but I won't like it."

The real trouble was that even Dad

didn't think much of his sister's family whom they would be visiting. Most Neanderthal folk lived in tribes who made their homes in caves. During the Ice Age, life was very hard indeed, and neighbours who could help each other in times of trouble were essential. With water being drawn from the river, firewood being chopped, flints being chipped and all the bustle and activity of a Neanderthal living place going on from dawn to dusk, life was hectic. Which was how people liked it. Most of them, that is. For there were families who lived in remote places far from their nearest neighbours.

That was how Littlenose's Uncle Juniper and his family lived. Littlenose had never met them but he knew that their home was far away in the mountains where the juniper bushes grew. Juniper berries were prized as medicine by the Neanderthal doctors, and every autumn the people of the mountains brought the season's fruit down to market. Littlenose's uncle was one of the best known, which accounted for his name. This much Littlenose had been told, but he had heard much more while lying awake at night listening to Mum and Dad talking.

"How can anyone live like that?" said Dad. "They do nothing. They see nothing. A crowd of yokels. Hill-billies. You can't even get decent conversation out of them. When I met Juniper at the market last week he hardly said a word from first to last."

"He probably couldn't get a word in edgeways," said Mum. "And he did say enough to invite us all to stay. In any case, if you don't like them why did you accept?"

"I wasn't thinking," groaned Dad. "I thought they only wanted Littlenose."

Next morning, after breakfast, Mum began the task of sorting out what they would need on holiday. Littlenose laid out his spear, his fire-making flints and his lucky coloured stone, and said, "I'm ready." But to his disgust Mum made him pack several pairs of clean furs as well. Looking at the mound of baggage, Dad said, "I think we might have been quicker just wrapping up the whole cave. We *are* only going to be away for three weeks, not the rest of our lives."

It was just getting light when they loaded Two-Eyes and set off next day. Uncle Juniper's home was one week's march due east of their own cave, and Dad explained that if they walked with the rising sun in their faces and camped at evening with the setting sun at their backs they couldn't go wrong.

On the second day out, Dad decided that they weren't travelling fast enough and had better break camp much earlier the following day. He roused everyone while it was still pitch dark, and set off. As they stumbled through the gloom, Mum said,

"You're quite sure we're going the right way?"

"Am I in the habit of making mistakes?" said Dad.

Mum just sniffed, while Littlenose nodded silently.

Then the sun rose . . . far to the left.

Dad stopped and muttered something which nobody could make out, but which seemed to imply that the sun was in the wrong place. But they changed direction, and went on their way.

On the fourth day Dad said, "We'll soon meet Uncle Juniper. When we stop tomorrow evening the sun should set exactly between two peaks. We have to wait at the pass between the peaks for Juniper to guide us the rest of the way."

Next evening as they made camp

Littlenose watched the rim of the setting sun slip down between two sharp mountain tops. Before the light had completely gone Dad scratched a mark on the ground like a spear pointing towards the pass where tomorrow they hoped to find Uncle Juniper.

In fact Uncle Juniper found *them* next morning as they rested by a clear spring, and they arrived at the Juniper family cave before dusk.

It was very similar to the one in which

Littlenose lived, with one marvellous difference. His cousins had a cave of their own, a smaller one that opened off the family cave. Here he was tucked up for the night with the three other boys, but none of them wanted to sleep. They whispered together in the dark exchanging boy-news. Littlenose told them of his home by the big river, of his visits to the market and his hunting lessons. He told them of bears and hyenas and sabre-toothed tigers. His cousins listened with amazement to the long stories of all his adventures. Then he asked, "What do *you* do around here?"

After a long pause, one cousin said, "Throw stones."

After another, even longer, pause the second cousin said, "Gather berries."

After a pause that was so long that

Littlenose thought he had fallen asleep the third cousin said, "Throw more stones."

Littlenose's heart sank. This holiday was going to be every bit as dull as he imagined!

Next morning, after breakfast, Littlenose said, "What shall we do?" Without replying, his cousins stuck a row of sticks in the ground at the end of a stretch of green turf . . . and started to throw stones at them. They were very good at it, which Littlenose wasn't. They knocked the sticks flying every time, but Littlenose found that he could not even throw far enough, let alone straight and hard enough. Apart from the occasional squabble, they threw stones all that day. And the next. And the next. Littlenose was frantic with boredom, and his throwing arm ached. Then, he remembered the other thing his cousins did. "What about going berry picking?" he asked at lunch. His aunt looked up. "Yes," she said, "I could do with some blaeberries, but remember, don't go past the cairns." The cousins nodded. Littlenose didn't know what a cairn was, but he nodded too.

The berry picking was, if anything, more boring than the stone throwing. There were very few berries, and soon Littlenose's back ached from stooping. He straightened up, and saw a promising blaeberry patch some way off. He was going towards it when he heard a shout from the other boys: "Not past the cairn!" He waved and walked on, and they shouted again. Then he saw a huge heap of large stones, as tall as he was. Other heaps were in a long line across the hillside. These must be the cairns.

He shrugged and turned back. "Why?"
he asked. His cousins looked at each other
and mumbled something that sounded like
"bigfoot".

"Who's Bigfoot?" asked Littlenose. But
his cousins wouldn't explain and just
hurried back to the cave.

After supper, Dad took Littlenose to one
side and said, "I hope you haven't been
upsetting your cousins. The folk in these

parts are simple and superstitious. They say if you go past the line of stone cairns the local bogey man will grab you." Dad grinned. "He's tall, hairy, and you can smell him a long way off. And he leaves enormous footprints." Littlenose grinned back at Dad. It sounded very fanciful, but still the line of cairns was intriguing. He made up his mind to explore beyond them, if only to show his simple cousins that there was nothing to be afraid of.

Next morning, before anyone was awake, Littlenose crept from the cave and made his way to the blaeberry place. The early-morning mist made it difficult to see, and he groped his way carefully forward. Suddenly he stopped. A tall shape loomed in front of him and his hair stood on end with fright. But the figure didn't move.

Then the mist thinned in the breeze and he saw that it was one of the stone cairns. Sighing with relief, Littlenose pressed on.

The mist rolled away completely with the coming day, and he found himself crossing a steep, bare mountainside covered with stunted trees and scrubby bushes. Patches of last winter's snow lay here and there, and Littlenose was scanning the ground ahead when he noticed something odd about one of the patches. There were huge footprints on it. But they were old. The edges were blurred where the sun had melted the snow, and the more he looked at them the less sure he became that they *were* footprints. All the talk of Bigfoot was making his eyes play tricks on him. He went on his way.

Then he stopped at another snow patch.

Here there were more marks like the last. But these were fresh, and most definitely footprints. Something very big had passed in front of him only a short time before!

For the second time, Littlenose's hair stood on end. His mind went numb and he couldn't think. He jumped at a sudden sound. Something was coming out of the bushes . . . In the split second before he

took to his heels, Littlenose had a glimpse
of something tall, shaggy and man-shaped
looming out of the dark undergrowth.
Littlenose flew downhill over snow, rock
and gravel. Behind him the thing shambled
swiftly in pursuit, plodding rapidly on
enormous feet and short, powerful legs.
And it was gaining on him.

The giant creature took one stride for
every three of Littlenose's. He knew that he
could never outrun it, but if he could hide,
Dad or Uncle Juniper would come looking
for him. There was a dead tree straight
ahead. It had been struck by lightning and
stood white and bare against the dark green
scrub. Littlenose ran the last few steps, and
dragged himself up to safety.

From his branch Littlenose looked down
on the creature. It was twice as tall as a

man, covered with shaggy fur, and had small eyes and a wide mouth with jagged teeth. And there was a terrible smell – like dead animals and damp caves all jumbled together. There was no mistake – this was Bigfoot!

When Bigfoot reached the tree he grabbed the trunk and shook it hard, roaring with all his might. Littlenose shook like a leaf in a gale, while Bigfoot tried to climb after him. But the lower branches weren't strong enough and broke under his weight.

As he clung to the tree, Littlenose began to think. It might be a long time before anybody came to his rescue, and it seemed unlikely that the dead tree would stand much of Bigfoot's shaking. He had to do something before the whole lot crashed to

the ground. He rummaged furiously in his furs and fished out his fire-making flints. Animals were afraid of fire and Bigfoot was at least part animal. Quickly he struck a spark on to the dead leaves clinging to a withered branch. The leaves caught fire and the branch became a torch. Breaking it off, Littlenose leaned forward and carefully dropped the flaming branch. But Bigfoot sidestepped, and as the burning torch fell to the ground picked it up and threw it into the bushes.

"He's not all *that* animal," thought Littlenose in dismay. There seemed no point in lighting another branch, and he looked around in despair for a new idea. Then he realised that Bigfoot's attention had wandered. He was sniffing loudly, and swinging his head from side to side.

Littlenose saw that a grey pall of smoke was blowing across the hillside. The torch had set fire to the undergrowth. The smoke became thicker, and swirled around the foot of the tree until Bigfoot was only a dim, coughing shape. This was Littlenose's chance. He slithered to the ground, and under cover of the smoke ran as fast as he could. Behind him he heard thudding footsteps as Bigfoot took up the chase again. But now Littlenose could see the line of the cairns.

He passed the first cairn and glanced over his shoulder. Bigfoot was almost on him. Then he heard a voice: "Get down, Littlenose!" And at the same something whizzed past his ear. Littlenose threw himself flat and heard Bigfoot roaring angrily behind him. Raising his head he saw a shower of well-aimed stones flying through the air while Bigfoot tried to fend them off with wildly waving arms.

At last the monstrous creature gave up and stumbled back up the mountainside and out of sight, leaving behind a trail of huge footprints and a dreadful smell. The cousins threw their remaining stones for luck before escorting Littlenose back to the cave.

The grown-ups weren't told of his adventure.

As he was leaving with Dad, Mum and Two-Eyes at the end of the holiday, Uncle Juniper said to Littlenose, "Well, and how would you like to live here with us in peace and quiet?"

"Actually," replied Littlenose, "I think the excitement would be too much for me. Goodbye, and thank you for having me."

100,000 YEARS AGO people wore no clothes. They lived in caves and hunted animals for food. They were called NEANDERTHAL.

50,000 YEARS AGO when Littlenose lived, clothes were made out of fur. But now there were other people. Littlenose called them Straightnoses. Their proper name is HOMO SAPIENS.

5,000 YEARS AGO there were no Neanderthal people left. People wore cloth as well as fur. They built in wood and stone. They grew crops and kept cattle.

1,000 YEARS AGO towns were built, and men began to travel far from home by land and sea to explore the world.

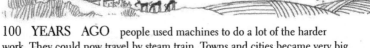

500 YEARS AGO towns became larger, as did the ships in which men travelled. The houses they built were very like those we see today.

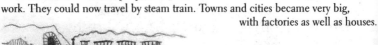

100 YEARS AGO people used machines to do a lot of the harder work. They could now travel by steam train. Towns and cities became very big, with factories as well as houses.

TODAY we don't hunt for our food, but buy it in shops. We travel by car and aeroplane. Littlenose would not understand any of this. Would YOU like to live as Littlenose did?